D0054291

STERLING and the distinctive Sterling logo are registered
trademarks of Sterling Publishing Co., Inc.

Library of Congress Cataloging-in-Publication Data

Le Gall, Pierre.
 [Constance et Miniature. English]
 Constance and Tiny / by Pierre Le Gall and Éric Héliot ;
[English translation by Shannon Rowan and Robert Agis].
    p. cm. -- (Constance)
 Summary: Constance thinks that her parents are evil,
so she runs away with her beloved cat Tiny.
 ISBN 978-1-4027-6648-0
 [1. Cats--Fiction. 2. Runaways--Fiction. 3. Parent and child--Fiction.]
 I. Héliot, Eric, ill. II. Rowan, Shannon. III. Agis, Robert. IV. Title.
 PZ7.L4537Co 2009
 [E]--dc22                                    2008047455

10 9 8 7 6 5 4 3 2 1

Originally published in France under the title *Constance et Miniature*
© 2007 Hachette Livre
English translation by Shannon Rowan and Robert Agis.
English translation copyright © 2009 Sterling Publishing Co., Inc.

Published in 2009 by Sterling Publishing Co., Inc.
387 Park Avenue South, New York, NY 10016
Distributed in Canada by Sterling Publishing
c/o Canadian Manda Group, 165 Dufferin Street
Toronto, Ontario, Canada M6K 3H6
Distributed in the United Kingdom by GMC Distribution Services
Castle Place, 166 High Street, Lewes, East Sussex, England BN7 1XU
Distributed in Australia by Capricorn Link (Australia) Pty. Ltd.
P.O. Box 704, Windsor, NSW 2756, Australia

Printed in China in January 2009
All rights reserved

Sterling ISBN 978-1-4027-6648-0

For information about custom editions, special sales, premium and
corporate purchases, please contact Sterling Special Sales Department
at 800-805-5489 or specialsales@sterlingpublishing.com.

# CONSTANCE
## and
## Tiny

by
Pierre Le Gall and Éric Héliot

STERLING

New York / London

My name is Constance.
I am locked up in an evil mansion.

It's my parents' house.
They are terrible people—
unfair and mean!

At dinner, they make me eat
disgusting food that stinks.

Every day, they take me to a school
where the teachers torture me.

And even when I try my best,
they are never happy.

No matter what I do, my room is
never clean enough.

In fact, nothing I do
is *ever* good enough for them.

I try to talk to them,
but it doesn't do any good.
They never listen to me.

Fortunately, I have a friend.
He's my cat, Tiny.
He's so sweet and gentle.

We can play for hours and
hours without stopping,
just the two of us.

But my parents hate Tiny,
even though my poor little kitty
wouldn't hurt a fly.

So, one day, I quietly
packed up my suitcase.

And I tucked poor
little Tiny under my arm.

What luck!
I found some money,
just lying alone in a corner.

Then I escaped from my prison
and ran as far away as possible.

Free at last!

Thanks to the money I found,
we were able to live quietly
for a little while.

But my parents hired a couple
of bandits to capture us.

They dragged us to their hideaway.
Tiny was terrified.

My parents came to get us.
Right then I knew that the horrors
were far from over.

First they tried to suffocate me.

Then they hauled us back
to their evil mansion.

Poor Tiny. Poor me.
We were prisoners again.
But only until I hatch a new plan.

It's exhausting being good
all the time!

[5]